G000092828

Old Sayings and Crazy Metaphors

Some are very old and some are new. I bet
you heard a lot of them and used a few.

By

Janice C Gentry

Copyright © May 8, 2020

Janice C Gentry

I'm dedicating this book to my Granddaughters, JaNiyha, Leah, JaShyia and Jannah. They gave me the idea to put this little book of sayings together.

The sayings are in no special order, I just wrote them down as I thought of them or when I heard one.

These are what you would hear your parents, grandparents, neighbors and other people say. Some are wise, crazy, weird or just funny.

I'll sleep when I'm dead.

You have diarrhea of the mouth and constipation of the brain.

Poor Henry, he's taking a dirt nap.

Love might be blind but the neighbors aren't.

The toes you step on today may be connected to the foot in your ass tomorrow.

She can start an argument with herself.

That makes about as much sense as tits on a bull.

I'll slap you to sleep, then slap you for sleeping.

That old dog won't hunt.

The grass is always greener on the other side of the fence.

You couldn't carry a tune if you had a bucket with a lid on it.

Keep on you will learn.

I reckon.

The grass may be greener on the other side of the fence, but that means it just thicker and harder to mow.

Whistling girls and crowing hens are bound to come to no good end.

You would rather run thru hell with gasoline drawer on, than to piss me off.

Why put gas in a car that's sitting in the junk yard.

You can't ride two horses with one ass.

Her mouth runs like a boarding house toilet.

You don't have two pennies to rub together.

Common sense not that common after all.

Jumping out the frying pan into the fire.

Look before you leap.

One who does evil is studied by evil.

Who do you think I am, Sam Sausage Head?

You must be smellin yo self.

Don't try snatching ass.

Don't make me beat the devil out of you.

Don't make me smack fire out yo back

He got one of those bathroom whooping's.

Them kids so bad they would tear the devil and his house up.

You don't have a pot to piss in or a window to throw it out.

I brought you into this world and I will take you out.

I know you got some sayings.

You better eat my eatins

You'll catch more flies with honey than with vinegar.

Some nerve, the pot calling the kettle black.

I was born one day but it wasn't yesterday.

I was born at night, but not last night.

I see the Fuck-Up Fairy has visited us again!

Pretty is as pretty does.

To many cooks spoil the gravy.

Do I look like I have stupid written across my forehead?

Get them pants out your mailbox.

Don't judge a book by its cover.

If your friends jumped off the bridge are you going to jump too?

Put your brains in a bird and it would fly backwards.

I'll cut you as fine as a cat's hair.

It's better to have it and not need it, then to need it and not have it.

That's not clean, you only gave it a lick and a promise.

I'll cut your ass too short to shit.

Who you think you talking to, Boo Boo the fool?

Can't trust you no further than I can spit!

A watched pot never boils.

Can't trust you no further than I can throw you!

It's gonna rain my knees done swoll up.

Artha came for a visit today.

My get up and go just got up and went.

I can't smell no flowers if I'm dead.

You may not be watching nobody but somebody is always watching you.

You better learn how to cook cause it takes face powder to catch a man but baking powder to keep him!

If wishes were horses beggars would ride.

You can't hide shit, cause it stinks.

Fool me once, shame on you. Fool me twice, shame on me!

A penny saved is a penny earned.

Who's that devil knockin on my door.

Those prices higher than a giraffe's ass.

A hard head makes a soft ass.

You got too many irons in the fire.

They scarce as hen's teeth.

You never miss your water till your well run dry.

Don't make me no never-mind.

She's got more ass than a cow got tits.

Shut up before you be wearing 3 shoes.

One bad apple spoils the whole barrel.

A rolling stone gathers no moss.

A disobedient child days are shortened on this earth.

Your mouth is like a clatter bone in a goose's behind.

Stop looking in my mouth.

When you make your bed hard, you lay hard.

One man's trash is another man's treasure.

Don't put the cart before the horse.

You lay down with dogs, you get up with fleas.

Get on out doze!

Every shut eye ain't sleep. and every good bye ain't gone.

Stay in a child's place.

Don't put all your eggs in one basket.

You can lead a horse to water, but you can't make it drink.

I'll give you something to cry for!

Stop running in and out!! You letting flies in!

Don't look a gift horse in the mouth.

Don't cut off your nose to spite your face.

Lookin like who shot John.

Don't throw stone for stone.

Let sleeping dogs lie.

Everything that glitters ain't gold and everything that's said ain't to be told.

Don't let your mouth write a check your ass can't cash.

I'm 3 times 7, twice 11 and then some. Don't ask me my age again.

What's done in the night will come to light.

I can't stand a mannish child.

If she like it I love it.

Ain't nothing open this time of morning but legs.

The world is going to hell in a hand basket.

Do your best and God will do the rest.

When love is no longer being served, it's time to get your ass up from the table.

I liked to give that so and so a piece of my mind.

If you lie, you'll steal and sho might kill.

This ain't my first rodeo.

That don't cut the mustard.

Don't bite off more than you can chew.

Now, you know all his chairs don't pull up to the table.

Stop grinning like a Cheshire cat.

I'm so mad my asshole quiver.

Granny where we goin? Ta hell if ya don't pray.

Satan get behind me!

Yall smell like outdoors, go sit down somewhere.

That bear don't dance.

You can wish in one hand and shit in the other then see which one get filled first.

God protect babies and fools.

Two clean sheets can't get each other dirty.

You're making a mountain out of a mole hill.

If it ain't broke don't fix it.

Every tub sits on its own bottom.

Watch yo mouth and save yo teeth

If it was a snake it would've bite you right in the face.

Come on now either piss or get off the pot.

Seem like the more I teach you the dumber you get.

You a lie and the truth ain't in ya

She slow as molasses.

What's good for the goose is good for the gander.

I walked 5 miles up hill in the snow to get to school and twice that to get back home.

You wrong as two left shoes.

You fight them or you gonna fight me.

Got to go catch that mule.

That's water under the bridge

Walk on over here like you got another ass at home. I'll knock that one off, so you can go home and put that other one on.

You'll reap what you sow.

I'll tear your kingdom down.

It will be a cold day in Juvember before you get something from me again.

It's cold as a black witch heart outside.

A leaning tree ain't always the first to fall.

Don't let the door knob hit cha where the good Lord split cha.

You don't believe fat meat greasy?

If you never had bad times how will you know good times when it comes around.

Many hands make light work.

I'll tear your ass out the frame.

It was like herding cats.

If your brain was ink there wouldn't be enough to dot an i.

Shame upon you.

You make my ass wanna dip snuff.

The apple don't fall far from the tree.

Respect your elders.

Children should be seen and not heard.

Excuse yourself when grown folks are talking.

Take all you want but eat all you take.

I don't give a piss ant or a piss uncle, long as you don't piss on me.

Even a mule gets tired.

Better use some of that elbow grease.

I've forgotten more than you'll ever know.

Till the cows come home.

Oh, you think you grown now.

Smell between yo legs, do you smell like a women or little girl.

I'll slap the taste out yo Mouth.

You ain't worth what the buzzard left on the roof.

You don't believe shit stink til you smell it.

Birds of a feather flock together.

I'm gonna be on you like white on rice.

If you scared say you scared.

Don't buy a pig in a poke.

You lying like a throw rug.

I don't want to hear a rat walking on flour.

I better be able to hear a rat piss on cotton.

I can show you better than I can tell you.

Use your head for something other than a hat rack.

When you get your hands dirty, they don't always come clean.

"So, I see", said the blind man.

Trouble easy to get into but hard to get out of.

You look like dicky did when his daddy died.

You got more mouth than a cow got ass.

If you can't say anything nice don't say anything at all.

Your daddy not made of glass.

Be in the house before street lights come on.

Your mother could have saved us all a lot of trouble if she just swallowed.

I will bust your head down to the white meat!

Fast ass child.

Bring me a switch.

An empty wagon makes a lot of noise.

Shut the door you won't raised in a barn.

I'll slap you into next week.

Lord, that's somebody's child.

Who you think you talking to?

If they won't work, they will steal.

Sharp as a tack, rusty as a nail.

He nervous as a cat on a hot tin roof.

If you lie, you will cheat, and if you cheat you will steal.

Stop being manish.

You full of more crap than a Christmas turkey.

You acting hot in the ass.

Keep lying your tongue is gonna stick to the roof of your mouth.

I'll knock your eyeballs out and stomp them in the ground.

Look at Ruth her leg broke again (she's pregnant).

Turn that TV off while the Lord is working.

He's the dummy in the woodpile.

There're no more eggs in the hen house but there's still water in the well.

Mark my word.

I'll be on yo ass like a duck on a June bug.

Pay yourself first.

Don't put your purse on the floor, cause you'll always be broke

A squeaky wheel gets the grease.

Live your own life.

There're three sides to every story, yours, theirs and the truth.

I didn't just fall off a turnip truck.

I may act crazy but I'm not stupid.

I'm too old of a cat to be fooled by such a young kitten.

You might be slick, but you can stand one more greasing.

If you see me fighting a bear, don't help me, help the bear.

I've lost a many fights, but I've won even more. Now take your chances.

Smelling just like a pole cat

Play the hand that's dealt you.

Go take that bob tail dress off.

A bird in the hand is better than a thousand birds in the air.

Well I'll be good goddamn.
.
Quit chunking them rocks.

Wait til you have kids, you gonna see.

Actin like yo shit don't stink.

Knee high to a grass hopper.

You ain't worth two dead flies.

You got more nerve than Carter's got liver pills.

Keep on living you'll learn.

He's drunk as Cooter Brown.

A no-good man is just like a bus, there's always another one around the corner.

He's a booger bear.

Spare the rod spoil the child.

I will knock you in the middle of next week.

If you're not happy it's your own fault.

If, ifs and buts were candy and nuts Christmas would be every day.

I'll mop the floors up with you.

Plant you now, dig you later.

Robbing Peter to pay Paul.

I ain't gonna be with you always.

I wish you would!

Keep crying and I'll give you something to cry for.

That ain't putting no candy in the baby's mouth and it ain't paying for the one he just ate.

I'm not sleep. I'm just resting my eyes.

The funny thing about young fools is they always turn out to be old fools.

What do you think, I'm chewing paper and shitting out dollar bills.

Give a dog enough rope he'll soon hang himself.

Getting old ain't for sissies.

What's that got to do with the price of potatoes?

You're standing out like a fly in buttermilk.

When you get grown, you're going to wish you was a child again.

Something from nothing leaves nothing, and you don't get something unless you work for it.

A clean conscience makes a soft pillow.

Always ask. They can only say no.

Be nice to people on the way up, as you will meet them on the way down.

You don't have to go home, but you got to get the hell outa here.

Can't never could.

You may not be hitting it, but you're sure scaring-the-hell out of it.

You don't get something for nothing.

Cleanliness is next to godliness.

Sometimes you gotta call a spade a spade and other times you gotta call it a shovel.

Don't buy what you can't afford.

I cried because I had no shoes until a met a man who had no feet.

Actions speak louder than words.

You looking for sympathy? Look in the dictionary between 'shit' and 'syphilis'.

19

A watched pot never boils.

It is morally wrong to let a fool keep their money.

Remember the history books are written by the winners.

It ain't illegal if you don't get caught.

I'd rather owe it to you than cheat you out of it.

If it's free, it's worth-less.

A lock only keeps an honest man honest.

Everyone going somewhere but ain't nobody going nowhere.

Every dog has his day and the puppies have the weekend.

It will all come out in the wash.

Stop wearing your heart on your sleeve.

A dog that bring a bone will carry a bone.

Eat all your food cause there's hungry people in China.

Don't throw the rock then hide your hand.

It's a poor rat that only has one hole.

Money don't grow on trees.

I will light you up like a Christmas tree.

You're rotten to the core.

Don't shit where you eat.

Hee hee hell.

That bread stale as your ass.

Is a frog's ass watertight?

Stop draggin your wagon.

He's three sheets to the wind.

All kinfolk ain't kin and every person with a grin ain't your friend.

You can't miss what you can't measure.

An eye for an eye and a tooth for a tooth will leave a world full of blind toothless fools.

The road to hell is paved with good intentions.

You can't have your cake and eat it too.

When God close a door, he opens a window.

He's a piss poor excuse for a man.

Don't let your bad deeds come back and bite you in the ass.

The sun shines on a dog's ass once in a while.

It's hot as fish grease.

She laughed so hard tears ran down her legs.

I ain't seen you in a month of Sundays.

Shit fire, and save the matches.

Keep me near the cross.

The biggest mistake you could ever make is being afraid to make one.

You smell like six miles of mule shit.

Sit down when you eat. You standing makes the house look poor.

He so skinny. He ain't nothing but breath and britches.

The cow gonna need its tail when fly time come.

A heap of people see things but only a few know what's happening.

The writing's on the wall.

Ain't nothing in the drugstore that can kill you faster than me.

If you don't get old you die young.

Jealousy is a disease. Get well soon Bitch!

The more you cry the less you piss.

The early birds get the worm.

If you spent less time complaining about your life, maybe you would enjoy it more.

This Louisville slugger will knock you out.

Little pitchers have big ears.

If the handwriting is on the wall, you're in the toilet.

No matter how many times a snake shed its skin, it will always be a snake.

To know better is to do better.

His hair is dyed, fried and laid to the side.

You only have one time to raise your children. Don't take any wooden nickels.

Snakes don't hiss anymore, they call you babe, bro and friend.

This to shall pass.

Tell the truth and shame the devil.

You're phony as a three-dollar bill.

Shame in the face, bold in the ass.

Oh! he dressed casket sharp.
.

Before I ask him for something I'll sleep in the street and peck shit with the birds.

Be careful of the hole you dig for someone else; you might just fall in it.

A new broom sweeps clean, but oh how that ole broom knows those corners.

If you go out there looking for trouble, you gonna find it.

The only friend you got is the dollars in yo pocket.

Stop popping that gum like a street walker!

Money can't buy you love but it sure makes a great down payment.

You look rode hard and put away wet.

Bless her heart!

He'll steal the ginger out of ginger bread.

Even a broke clock is right twice a day.

One day you gona put your hand on something and get it cut off.

Ain't never been a bird that flew so high it didn't have to come down to eat.

I'm not made of money!

You ain't got no back; you got a gristle.

She's stirring the mustard.

Heap sees and few knows.

That coffee is as strong as Jack Johnson.

When you throw mud, you leave dirt on your hands.

You can't make a silk purse out of a sow's ear.

She givin it away outta both panty legs.

I wouldn't give him the time of day.

You can tell me where you been, but you can't tell me where you're going.

I'll snatch a knot in your ass the doctor can't get out.

I was hungrier than a big dog.

So what, it's raining, you ain't gona melt.

Make sure you put on clean underwear.

Your ass is grass and I'm the lawn mower.

Why lie when the truth will do.

Crazier than a outhouse rat.

Right ain't never wronged nobody.

A steady drop of water will melt a rock.

Don't question my word, if I tell you a duck can pull a truck all you need to do is just hitch it up.

You a day late and a dollar short.

He's as old as Methuselah.

Don't count your chickens before they hatched.

God don't like ugly.

His bread ain't done.

Why buy the cow when you can get the milk free?

That boy got a lil sugar in his tank.

What does that have to do with the price of tea in China?

It doesn't matter what they call you, what matters is what you answer to.

You was born alone and you gona die alone.

You can't beat that with a stick.

A little bit of something beats a whole lot of nothing.

He too lazy to work in a pie shop.

No fools, no fun.

If it ain't rats, it's roaches.

It's not in back of you it's in front of you.

Don't piss on my leg and tell me it's raining!

I'm slow, but sure.

Don't get to big for yo britches.

He'll steal a nickel off a dead's man eye.

Who don't hear in their ear, will feel in their ass?

27

You'd better shut up before your people be wearing black and walking slow.

You trying to live a champagne life with beer money.

There may be snow on the roof but there's still fire in the furnace.

I'm gonna fix your little red wagon.

You a lie, and the truth ain't in you.

All whores don't walk the streets.

What goes around comes around.

You can't hoot with the owls at night and expect to soar with the eagles in the morning.

You lie at the bat of an eye.

He who thinks by the inch and acts by the foot should be removed from my yard.

There's a dead cat on the line somewhere.

I got mine and Captain Jack got his.

When you think by the inch and talks by the yard you deserve to be kicked by the foot.

If I had a nickel for every time I heard that I'd be rich.

Don't let your right hand know what your left hand is doing.

It's hot as a firecracker.

One monkey don't stop no show.

He's sharp as a tack.

Child you ain't got a back; you got gristle.

The deed ain't proof of possession, and the lease ain't proof of ownership.

I will knock you in the middle of next week.

I'll slap the taste out of your mouth.

I rather die on my feet than live on my knees.

Don't get beside yourself.

A son is a son till he takes him a wife, a daughter is a daughter all of her life.

What y'all doing. Y'all to quite in there.

You rubbing salt in the wound.

What the daughter does, the mother did.

She's pitching a hissy fit.

When I say jump, you ask how high.

He's a snake in the grass.

Stop running around like a chicken with his head cut off.

Walk like you got somewhere to go.

That stick you using, I threw it away long time ago.

Tough row to hoe.

Don't try to play me.

You mad? Then scratch your ass and get glad.

You got as much chance of winning as a one-legged man in an ass kickin contest.

I feel like I've been chewed up and spit out.

Mind your P's and Q's.

Do as I say, not as I do.

When I was your age, we didn't have all these crazy toys.

What part of "no" don't you understand?

Who put a bee in your bonnet?

If you don't stop making faces, it's going to freeze that way.

If you can't run with the big dogs, stay under the porch.

He was as nervous as a long-tailed cat in a room full of rocking chairs.

It's colder than a penguin's balls.

He ain't got the sense God gave a goose.

I wouldn't walk across the street to piss on him if he was on fire.

I'll knock you so hard you'll see tomorrow today.

He can't find his ass with both hands in his back pockets.

If his lips movin he's lying.

Quit goin' around your ass to get to your elbow.

I'm so broke I can't afford to pay attention.

You don't know shit from shinola.

That skirt was so tight I could see her religion.

You're so full of shit your eyeballs are brown.

It's drier than popcorn fart.

You so dumb, you don't know whether to check your ass or scratch your watch.

That lazy bum won't hit a lick at a snake.

You're lyin' like a no-legged dog.

He's so dumb, he could throw himself on the ground and miss.

If that boy had an idea, it would die of loneliness.

Keep it up and I'll cancel your birth certificate.

She so dumb she couldn't pour piss out of a boot with the instructions.

He smelled bad enough to gag a maggot.

You better give your heart to Jesus, cause your ass is mine.

It happened faster than a knife fight in a phone booth.

He so ugly he'd scare a buzzard off a gut pile.

He ran outa there like a scalded dog.

He looks like ten miles of bad road.

If he were an inch taller, he'd be round.

It was colder than a witch's tit in a brass bra.

Hotter than blue blazes.

She dun gone and got all boo-gee on us.

Knowledge without wisdom is as dangerous as a fool with a loaded gun.

A fish wouldn't get caught if it kept it's mouth shut.

Everybody wants to go to heaven but nobody wants to die.

Money can buy anything but good sense.

Believe half of what you see and none of what you hear.

Going to church doesn't make you a Christian no more than standing in a corn field makes you corn.

"What you looking at!" "Shit to keep from stepping in it."

She's showing her true colors.

Tomorrow ain't promise to nobody.

An educated fool is a dangerous fool.

She kind of long in the tooth.

He kicking up his heels.

A leopard can't change his spots.

You need to slow your roll.

A little bird told me.

A hit dog will hollow.

Do you have eyes in the back of your head?

The blacker the berry the sweet the juice.

Be careful what you wish for you just might get it.

Beauty is only skin deep.

Don't burn your bridges behind you.

He's blind in one eye and can't see out of the other.

Can't live with them and can't live without them.

He's caught between a rock and a hard place.

Cold hands make a warm heart.

You couldn't hit the broad side of a barn.

Dead men tell no tales.

You digging your own grave.

The only way to be sure your two friends keep your secret is to kill both of them.

He ain't got a leg to stand on.

They will eat you out of house and home.

You don't need fair weather friend.

He's gonna go off all halfcocked.

God helps those who help themselves.

If you can't stand the heat, get out of the kitchen.

I got a bone to pick with you.

He's as crooked as a dog's hind leg.

If you can say huh' you can hear.

Why you eating so much? You got a tapeworm or something.

I don't trust him, he got beady eyes.

Only trash stays in the streets.

If he cheated with you, he will cheat on you.

Don't be sorry, be more careful.

You tell some, you keep some.

I feel a little peckish.

Don't get a wet ass and no cash.

You play with trash it gets in your eyes.

Don't fatten the fog for the snake.

A woman that is blessed is never involved in mess.

His ass aint worth a soup sandwich.

No, you not spinning the night at that fast tail girl's house!

I told you not to go nowhere and you dissa-damn-peared!

Don't go away mad just get the hell on.

I can show you better than I can tell you.

Opinions are just like assholes, everybody got one and they all stink.

Everybody loves a little ass; nobody loves a smart ass.

Common sense is anything but.

No good deed goes unpunished.

It's like horse shit – all over the place.

It's a poor craftsman who blames his tools.

He must be built backwards. his feet smell and his nose runs.

I'm gonna rip your arm off and beat you with the wet end.

You can't fix stupid.

Better an empty house than an unwanted guest.

Never miss a good opportunity to keep your mouth shut.

Sometimes you've gotta pull down your pants and slide on the ice.

If you fail to prepare, you're preparing to fail.

Never kick cow shit on a hot day.

Stop staring, take a picture it'll last longer.

The more you stir shit the worst it stinks.

Shake it don't break it, it takes nine months to make it.

I didn't hear you cause my eyes was shut.

She so ugly she cute.

If you big enough to hit, you big enough to get hit.

If you feelin a little foggy, then jump.

Put your money where your mouth is.

You always putting your foot in your mouth.

Don't throw stones if you live in a glass house.

Go ahead and try it, you just might like it.

The bigger they are, the harder they fall.

I'll cut off your head and shit down your neck

He's knee high to a short dog.

You don't know your ass from a hole in the ground.

Money talks, bull shit walks.

Your dumb ass can't walk and chew bubble gum at the same time.

Shit happens.

Tough titty said the kitty.

You always flapping your gums.

Shake it off.

God gave you two ears and one mouth for a reason.

If you kick a dog around too much he'll bite back.

He's up shitty creek without a paddle.

I don't have to do anything but stay black and die.

I got CRS (can't remember shit).

Cut to the chase.

There's no fool like an old fool.

I'm damned if I do and damned if I don't.

If you ain't crazy you doing a good job pretending.

He shitting in tall cotton.

Check yourself before you be by yourself.

It's my lie, I'll tell it anyway I want to.

What you mean we? I don't see but one of you.

Curiosity killed the cat.

Don't put all your eggs in one basket.

I rather be judged by twelve than carried by six.

A stiff dick has no conscious.

Close your mouth before you catch flies.

He's a jack of all trades and a master of none.

Leave well enough alone.

Don't bears shit in the woods?

You gotta fin for yourself.

Stop trying to blow smoke up my ass.

People in hell want ice water, and I'm not carrying a pitcher.

It's a low-down dirty shame.

You not worth the spit it takes to cuss you out.

You rather sandpaper a bobcat ass than to mess with me.

In those jeans her butt looks like two Buicks fighting for a parking space.

She was born short and slapped fat.

He looks like something the dog kept under the porch.

He wouldn't take the time to say shit if he had a mouth full of it.

The only way three people can keep a secret is if two of them are dead.

I'm not one of your lil friends.

First of all, check your tone.

I hope you know that school work like you know them songs.

You better take that bass out your voice

When we get in this store, don't ask for nothin and you better not touch nothin.

Fix your face before I fix it for you.

You fight them, or you fight me.

Cleanliness is next to Godliness.

Don't make me have to come in there!

I was built this way for a reason.

Caring for myself is not self-indulgence, it's self-preservation.

Absents make the heart grow fonder.

A raising tide lift all boats.

Make hay while the sun shine.

Beggars can't be choosy.

A thing of beauty is a joy forever.

You can't make an omelet without breaking a few eggs.

Don't throw the baby out with the bath water.

Early to bed, early to raise makes you healthy wealthy and wise.

Ain't no use crying over spilt milk.

You're a day late and a dollar short.

You're barking up the wrong tree.

He tells more lies than you can shake a stick at.

Share and share alike.

You're preaching to the choir.

Do it right or don't do it at all.

Always wear clean underwear in case you get in an accident.

Every dog has its day.

Hurry up we're burning daylight.

Where there's a will there's a way.

This is my yard now.

Let me see the back of your head get small

A little soap and water never killed anybody.

Are your hands put on backwards? Then pick up the phone some time

Don't cross your eyes or they'll get stuck that way.

I hope you don't kiss your mother with that mouth!

If I want your opinion, I'll ask for it!

If a bull frog had wings, he wouldn't bump his ass on the ground.

I'm gonna skin you alive!

Lie again and I'll smack you with the hand of Jesus.

There's enough dirt in those ears to grow potatoes!

When I was your age, I had to walk ten miles through the snow, uphill, both ways by myself, to go to school.

You had better wipe that smile off your face before you have to pick your lips up off the floor.

You don't always get what you want. It's a hard lesson, but you might as well learn it now.

That's a lie bump on your tongue.

The rumble strips on the side of the road are for blind drivers.

Keep swallowing gum and you'll shit rubber balls.

Just eat it. It taste like chicken.

When the ice cream truck plays the music, that means it's out of ice cream.

The dog went to live on a farm.

Sitting too close to the TV will ruin your eyesight.

If you swallow gum, it will stay in your stomach for 7 years.

Swallowing watermelon seeds will make a watermelon plant grow in your stomach.

No, you can't have any coffee it will stunt your growth.

The stork stopped by Auntie's house again.

There's no flies on her.

Who you gonna believe, me or your lying eyes?

It's blowing up a storm.

She's got gumption.

I found your nose, it was in my business again.

I heard it through the grape vine.

Karma's a real bitch.

Don't turn a blind eye.

I would slap you but shit splatters.

You on my stomping ground now.

You can't be the top dog if you act like a pussy!

Don't get caught with your pants down.

I will punch you by accident on purpose.

She's batshit crazy.

Yada, Yada, Yada.

You're beating a dead horse.

It's like looking for a needle in a haystack.

He's on a wing and a prayer.

Some time you have to fight fire with fire.

He's fast as grease lighting.

That just went over like a lead balloon.

You give me the heebie jeebies.

She's the real McCoy.

That's my story and I'm sticking to it.

Don't call the world dirty because you forgot to clean your glasses.

Everyone is entitled to be stupid, but some abuse the privilege.

Nowadays, legs spread quicker than rumors.

It's no skin off my back.

There's no rest for the wicked.

She's stirring up a hornet's nest.

I'm like fine wine I just get better with time.

You still wet behind the ears.

It ain't over til the fat lady sings.

Did you wake up on the wrong side of the bed?

He's always rubbing me the wrong way.

Don't pull any punches.

That's wishful thinking.

We can be alone together.

The easiest way to eat crow is warm because the colder it gets the harder it is to swallow.

Sometimes you get and sometimes you get got.

You're going to be eating crow before the nights out.

Expecting the unexpected make the unexpected expected.

Tell you not to do something and you turn around and do it twice and take pictures.

If the grass is greener on the other side, you can bet the water bill is higher.

A lie will make it around the world before the truth has time to put on its shoes.

You're only young once, but you can be an old fool over and over.

The best things in life either makes you fat, drunk or pregnant.

Common sense is like deodorant, the ones who need it most don't use it.

There are 70 ways to keep a man happy. One is alcohol, the rest is 69

You can't spell families, without "lies".

If you don't want a sarcastic answer, don't ask a stupid question.

Not all cute guys have girlfriends, a lot of them have boyfriends.

I would never jump in front of a bullet for somebody. If I have time to jump, they have time to jump the hell out of the way.

Don't bite the hand that feed you.

Sex education may be a good idea in the schools, but I don't believe the kids should be given homework.

It's a short distance from love to hate.

The squeaky wheel doesn't always get the grease, sometimes it just gets replaced.

Women and rocks are very much alike. We skip the flat ones.

I'm not bossy I just know what you should be doing.

If your aunt had balls, she'd be your uncle.

Come hell or high water.

He met a fate worse than death.

I wouldn't touch that with a ten-foot pole.

They from the wrong side of the track.

Life is too short to let people get away with the same shit.

A bird in the hand is worth two in the bush.

Don't shoot the messenger.

Now put that in your pipe and smoke it.

He's blowing the whistle.

That company is cooking their books.

Love many, trust few and always paddle your own canoe.

Life's a bitch then you die.

Don't butter my butt and call me a biscuit.

You got caught red handed.

Blood is thicker than water.

Go somewhere with those crocodile tears.

Close but no cigar.

Stop pulling my leg.

Let the chips fall where they may.

I got a mind like a steel trap.

Well, he's not the sharpest tool in the draw.

There's more to it than meets the eye.

That's a tough nut to crack.

You got a wild hair up your ass?

He's lying out of his ying yang.

That's dirty water under a new bridge.

That's a bald face lie.

She's the fuzz on my peach.

Now you cooking with gas.

The early bird gets the worm

You can stuff your "sorry" in a sock and stick it.

Go on with that foolishness.

The baby was born asleep.

This generation is weaker but wiser.

She's taking her last carriage ride.

Nothing beats a failure like a try.

It's bad enough that they think you're an idiot, you don't have to open your mouth to prove it.

You're not a smartass you're just as an ass and dumb.

I may love to shop but I'm certainly not buying any of that bullshit you trying to sell.

I can only explain it to you, I sure can't understand it for you.

Surprise me, say something intelligent.

If brains were dynamite you wouldn't be able blow your nose.

Your looney toon ass.

Silents is golden.

One day, you gonna choke on the shit you talk.

Act like your hairline and recede.

Necessity is the mother of invention.

You can't win a battle with somebody who is at war with themselves.

While the early bird gets the worm, the second mouse gets the cheese.

War determines who is left, not who's right.

Isn't it funny that in our neighborhood, pizza will get to your house faster that the police?

He's as slippery as an eel.

He's a couch potato in the gravy bowl of life.

Success has such a sweet smell.

Information travels faster in this modern age as our days start crawling away.

Politicians and diapers should be changed regularly, because they are both full of shit.

Calling you stupid would be an insult to stupid people.

Life has a tendency to come back and bite you in the ass.

Is your ass jealous of the amount of shit that just came out of your mouth?

Sometimes life is like a bicycle riding downhill.

You've always been swimming in the shallow end of the talent pool.

If you're gonna be two faced, at least make one of them pretty.

Keep rolling your eyes, maybe you'll find a brain back there.

Your family tree must be a cactus because everybody on it is a prick.

I can always tell when you're lying. Your lips are moving.

It looks like your face caught on fire and someone tried to put it out with a hammer.

What language are you speaking? Cause it sounds like bullshit.

I'd like to see things from your point of view, but I can't seem to get my head that far up your ass.

It's so cute when you try to talk about things you don't understand.

Love is like a fragile flower, if not taken care of properly it will wither and die to soon.

Karma takes too long; I'd rather beat your ass now.

If I wanted to hear from an asshole, I'd fart.

Just because you have an ass don't mean you have to act like one.

You are living proof that shit can sprout legs and walk.

I'm a pacifist, I'm about to pass a fist right across your face.

If bullshit could float, you'd be the captain of a boat.

The grass is always greener on the other side because it is fertilized with bullshit.

You trippin like big clown shoes.

You a lie and a wink and your asshole stink.

You'll never be the man your mother was.

Roses are red, Violets are blue. I've got five fingers, the middle one is for you.

You're about as useless as an asshole with taste buds.

When I look into your eyes, I see straight through to the back of your head.

He's as sharp as a bowling ball.

You're so short when you smoke weed you don't get high.

You're IQ's lower than your shoe size.

Act your age not your shoe size.

He's a few clowns short of a circus.

She's so ugly she has to sneak up on a mirror.

Your hairline is like Pluto, unreachable.

If you don't know you better ask somebody.

Don't sweat the small stuff.

Once your heart's been broken it grows back bigger and meaner.

Slow and steady wins the race

Think twice before you speak.

I don't know which face to talk to, since you have two of them.

Speak softly and carry a big stick.

Don't talk the talk if you can't walk the walk.

A mother is only as happy as her saddest child.

I can't tell if you're on too many drugs or not enough.

Your lips keep moving, but I don't hear a word you say.

Wipe your mouth, there's still a tiny bit of bullshit around your lips.

My name West, I ain't in that mess

I hate it when ugly people say "I need my beauty sleep." They need to hibernate.

Oh, what was that? I couldn't hear you though all that shit you talking.

There may be two sides to every story, but you're still a jackass in both of them.

Who pissed in your cornflakes this morning?

Knuck up if you buck up.

Don't start nothing it won't be nothing.

If you didn't see it with your own eyes or hear it with your own ears, don't invent it with your small mind and share it with your big mouth!

I hope you have life insurance, if you keep talking, you're gonna need it.

Your name Andy Pandy, eat shit and thought it was candy.

Twinkle twinkle little snitch, mind your own business you nosy bitch.

You thought like Lit, thought he had to piss but he shit.

You need to go brush your teeth cause all you seem to do is talk shit!

You started with nothing and still have most of it left.

My phone battery lasts longer than your relationships.

Two wrongs don't make a right.

Cleaning the house while the kids are home is like shoveling snow while it's still snowing.

Nice try, but you got the wrong guy.

If it sounds too good to be true, it probably is.

A bald spot is like a lie, the bigger it is the harder it is to cover it up.

Homie don't play that.

Men are like public toilets. The good ones are taken, the rest are full of shit.

If you were on fire and I had water I would drink it.

You're about as useful as a bucket without a bottom.

Even if you were twice as smart, you'd still be stupid!

Camping is spending a lot of money to live like somebody who is poor.

The enemy of my enemy is my friend.

He slithered into your life quietly so nobody would notice he was destroying it.

Gossip is a beast fed by those who repeat it.

A relationship without trust is like a cell phone without service. All you can do is play games.

You think you slick but you're just greasy.

If I was a dog, and you were a flower, I'd lift up my leg, and give you a shower.

If someone hates you for no reason, give that sucker a reason.

I hate two-faced people. It's so hard to decide which face to slap first.

I don't have a drinking problem, I'm just thirsty all the time.

Once again, you show all the sensitivity of a blunt axe.

He who takes offense when no offense is intended is a fool.

Anyone who helps you to gossip about someone can also help someone to gossip about you.

If you can't say anything nice, at least have the decency to be vague.

You're a pig and I don't allow livestock in the house.

A knife wound can heal, but a tongue wound can last forever.

Good girls are bad girls that never got caught.

It's not the insult that hurts, it's the truth in it that causes the pain.

Never use a big word when a little filthy one will do.

Being polite to a person is not a sign of respect, it's a sign of a good upbringing.

Insult can be disguise as compliment if embellished with flowery words.

I've never found the truth an insult, it's the liars who find it insulting.

Oh, what a tangled web we weave, when first we practice to deceive.

Sometimes the meanest thing that you can say about anyone is the truth.

If you take part in a discussion with a fool, then it two fools having a discussion.

Mama's baby, daddy's maybe.

Once is a mistake, twice is pattern, three times is a character flaw.

My name Bennett and I ain't in it.

Beware of a wolf in sheep clothing.

If you still from one person's work it's plagiarism, if you still from a lot of people's work it's research.

I'll slap you to sleep then slap you woke.

It's a joke as long as people are laughing, otherwise it's an insult.

If you chase two rabbits you end up losing both of them.

Never, under any circumstances, take a sleeping pill and a laxative on the same night.

A bank is a place that will lend you money, if you can prove that you don't need it.

Each insult has just enough truth in it to make it hurt.

If you want to add some variety to your sex life, why don't you just use your other hand?

The quickest way to point out your own weaknesses is to point out the weakness of others.

Beauty is only skin deep, but ugliness goes all the way to the bone.

The trouble with assuming is. it always starts with an ass.

A clear conscience is usually the sign of a bad memory.

It's not the fall that kills you; it's the sudden stop.

Never get into fights with ugly people, they have nothing to lose.

Hell, naw to the naw naw naw.

I'm rubber, you're glue, whatever you say bounce off me and sticks to you.

He fell off the wagon.

Money can't buy happiness, but it sure makes misery easier to live with.

If it's not etched in stone you can change it.

You can be the whole package and still end up at the wrong address.

You got a rubber neck, kiss your own ass.

The only thing necessary for evil to succeed is for good men to do nothing.

Don't hate appreciate.

Only with the power of love

An ounce of prevention is worth a pound of cure.

Silence equal complacency.

Keep talking about me behind my back, while God keep blessing me in front your face,

Just as sure as night follows day you will pay.

I taught you everything you know, but I didn't teach you everything I know.

Leave no stone unturned.

You'll never know where you're going if you don't know where you've been.

A fool and his money are soon parted.

That food so good I could smack yo Momma.

I'm so hungry my stomach is touching my back.

You got to stand for something or you will fall for anything.

Kick rocks.

You say what you mean and mean what you said.

To each his own.

A drunk man's tongue speaks a sober man's mind.

Two dead batteries can't jump each other.

If you think something small don't have an impact, try going to sleep with a mosquito in the room.

The proof is in the pudding.

If you hear hoof beats think horses.

Truth is like the sunshine; you can block it out for a while but it ain't going away.

He got beer muscles.

Don't bring a knife to a gun fight.

Nobody's free till everybody's free.

You can't help somebody who don't want help.

Stop dilly dallying around.

Let go of what was and have faith in what will be.

You can't make fresh lemonade with used lemons.

There is always a little truth behind every "just kidding".

Love held to loose will fly, love held to tight will die.

See one, do one, teach one.

You'll lie and a wink and your asshole stink.

There are two sides to every story.

I'll smack you so hard you'll hit the floor twice.

Whatever is good to you is most likely bad for you.

The quickest way to lose a friend is to loan them money.

I'm just saying.

What happens in Vegas stay's in Vegas.

You don't know that I know that you know that I know.

Don't try me, I'll put you in the trunk and then help look for you.

I'm sorry if common sense offends you.

I'm not always right but I'm never wrong.

It ain't over til it's over.

Old soldiers never die, they just fade away

You can see everything bad my kids do but you Ray Charles when it come to your kids.

Don't bite the hand that feed you when you're full then expect a hand out when you're starving again.

If you're persistent you will get it; if you're consistent you will keep it.

Every brick the enemy throw at you, use it to stand on.

Sorry for all the mean, hurtful, true things I said about you.

A true friend only post pictures you both look good in.

Don't lose a diamond while chasing glitter.

If you're already late take your time, you can't be late twice

I'm sick and tired of being sick and tired.

Rumors are carried by haters, spread by fools and accepted by idiots.

Always smell your money before you loan it out to make sure it not that "Lil funky ass 20" when you ask for it back.

Where there is smoke there's fire. If you ignore it you will get burned.

If not us then who? If not now than when?

Putting lipstick on a pig doesn't change the fact that it's a pig.

Bay Bay kids don't die, they just multiply.

Sometimes you can be your own worst enemy.

Sometimes people hate you because of the way other people love you.

Knowing someone and knowing of them are two totally different things, don't confuse the two.

Ain't nothing to it but to do it.

Sometimes you have to meet people where they are and sometimes you have to leave them there.

Don't start nothin and it won't be nothin.

You don't need to rule the world if you can rule the rulers.

You lie so much; I wouldn't believe you if you told me rain was wet.

All skin folk ain't kin folk.

My ego says "Once everything falls into place I'll find peace, The Spirit says "Find peace and everything will fall in place".

As long as I owe you, you'll never go broke.

You can't get blood from a turnup.

The reason I'm old and wise is because God protected me when I was young and dumb.

School those fools.

You can't go back and change the beginning, but you can start where you are and change the end.

If you're not at the table, you're on the menu.

Sometimes it's not a secret, it's just none of your business.

A pretty face gets old, a nice body will change, but a good woman stays a good woman.

I can't believe nothing you say, because I see what you do.

Don't trust words, trust actions. People can tell you anything but actions tell you everything.

Don't let your ice cream melt while you count somebody else sprinkles.

Same shit different toilet.

A narrow mind and a big mouth usually go together.

Suck it up, Buttercup.

Only a fool think you can cut 12 inches off the top of a blanket and sew it to the bottom then think you will have a longer blanket.

A child who reads will be an adult that thinks.

When the power of love overcomes the love of power, then the world will know peace.

I'll put you in a round room and make you sit in the corner.

Never give unlimited power to a person with a limited mind.

Pray for the best but prepare for the worst.

There is nothing more dangerous than an idiot with power who thinks he's a genius.

You can't make somebody love you by giving them more of what they already don't appreciate.

Throw me to the wolves and I will return the leader of the pack.

You'll continue to forgive the person you love until you hate them.

Arguing with a fool only proves there are two fools.

Great sex and the right lies will make a person waste year of their lives.

If the chase ain't mutual change directions.

Little secrets grow up to be big lies.

The highest level of leadership is to develop leaders, not gain followers.

Only when the last tree has died and the last river has been poisoned and the last fish has been caught will we realize that we can't eat money.

A snake draped in gold is still a snake.

Don't set yourself on fire to keep other people warm.

It does not matter where you start, it's where you finish that count.

If you want to lose a friend, let them move in.

If you pray for rain you got to deal with the mud.

There are two places you can stay for free, in your lane and out my business.

If you have a problem with me, call me. If you don't have my number that means you don't know me well enough to have a problem with me.

All snakes don't crawl, some walk right beside you.

You're dirt I wouldn't even walk on.

Don't let anybody who hasn't walked in your shoes tell you how to tie your shoelaces.

Don't put the key to your heart in somebody else's pocket.

In order for you to insult me, I must first value your opinion.

You can't find peace if you're the one causing all the hell.

Birds of a feather don't flock together when they are grown and have their own mind.

Those who stir the shit pot should have to lick the spoon.

Mean what you say and say what you mean.

Since light travels faster than sound, some people appear bright until you hear them speak.

I didn't say it was your fault, I said I was blaming you.

Behind every successful man is his woman. Behind the fall of a successful man is usually another woman.

You're never too old to learn something stupid.

The voices in my head may not be real, but they have some good ideas!

Why you driving this car like we got extra lives?

I will paint a house with a Q-tip before I worry about why you not speaking to me.

Life is like a toilet. There is always an asshole ready to shit on your day.

If it don't apply let it fly.

When a friend is going through a personal storm instead of being the weatherman and spreading the news, try being an umbrella and cover them with love.

There's a sucker born every minute and someone to take advantage of them every second.

They will turn on you for somebody who will turn on them.

The past is dead, the future is uncertain so the present is all you have.

He who dance with the devil will get surely get scorched.

If you have rolls, you better bet there's somebody that will butter them for you.

You don't look good when you try to make other people look bad.

The thing about getting old is, your eyelids get weaker but your ability to see though bullshit gets better.

When you hold grudges, your hands aren't free to catch blessings.

There are seven days in a week and Some Day isn't one of them.

Don't seek revenge. The rotten fruit will fall on its own.

The three great forces that rule the world are stupidity, fear and greed.

If you can't figure out how to be kind, then figure out how to be quiet.

The only keeper of your happiness is you.

The more you learn, the more you realize how much you don't know.

Being poor is a frame of mind, but being broke is only temporary.

The best source of knowledge is experience.

You can't fix somebody who don't want to be fixed, but you can ruin your life trying.

If only our tongues were made of glass, how much more careful we would be when we speak.

Before the truth can set you free, you need to recognize which lie is holding you hostage.

None of us sit so high we afford to look down on others.

Even if you don't speak it, the truth is the truth.

Guest are like fish, they start to stink after 3 days

If you play with a puppy, he will lick you in the mouth.

I'm not taking no bath! Water will rust iron and sink battleships.

We can't solve our problems with the same level of thinking that created them.

I'd rather swallow the bitter pill of truth than the sugar coated one of lies.

Always be trustful. Trust a snake to bite, a liar to lie, a cheater to cheat and a thief to steal.

If the shoe don't fit get another pair or go barefoot.

Get on your shit, stay on your shit, stay out of shit and don't tell people shit.

Insanity: doing the same thing over and over again and expecting different results.

You know you have a big heart when you feel bad for doing what's best for you.

If you're careless with the truth in small matters, you can't be trusted with important matters

When opportunity knocks, don't knock the opportunity.

Your argument is as clear as mud.

The measure of intelligence is the ability to change.

If things come easy and you get comfortable, you are getting trapped into dependency.

If you are a giver know your limits because takers don't have any.

A clever person solves a problem. A wise person avoids it.

If you want the best fruit sometimes you have to go out on a limb.

Nothing comes easily in life and if it comes easily, maybe it is not worth it.

Short term pleasures can lead to long-term traps.

Making the same mistake over and over hoping for a different outcome is a fool errand.

If you can't explain it to a six-year-old, you don't understand it yourself.

Don't curse your struggles, embrace them. They are your blessings in disguise.

Anyone who has never made a mistake has never tried anything new.

You can't simultaneously prevent a war and prepare for it

The tragedy of life is what dies inside a man while he's still alive.

If you remain silent about a wrong, you become guilty of complicity.

Yesterday's the past, tomorrow's the future, but today is a gift. That's why it's called the present.

Shut up before I kick you in the throat.

You're playing with my heart and it's getting pretty lame. Decide what you want; me or the game.

I'd kick you in the vagina but I don't wanna lose my shoe.

Whoever said money don't grow on trees obviously never sold weed.

The more you cry the less you piss.

I speak 4 languages: English, Profanity, Sarcasm, and Real shit.

Life moves pretty fast. If you don't stop and look around once in a while, you could miss it.

I will give you something to cry about!

Once you walk out of my life, the door locks behind you.

Don't get grown with me!

My heart is not a playground, so take your sorry ass somewhere else and play.

Success is the result of perfection, hard work and learning from failure.

I don't have to do anything but stay black and die.

Honey, I got heels higher than your standards.

Have you lost your rabbit ass mind?

If you judge me by my past, then you are totally behind schedule.

A wise person speaks carefully and with truth.

Oh, so you think I'm playing with you.

There are no ugly people; only ugly hearts.

You better be in the house before the street lights come on.

We must combine a tough mind and a tender heart to live a productive life.

Sorry I offended you when I called you a bitch, I had no idea you thought it was a secret.

You better be glad I know Jesus.

What will you get by doing what you are doing? If the answer is Nothing, then why do it?

You just like your damn daddy.

I used to think you took my breath away, then I realized I was suffocated by your bullshit.

I will pimp slap you so hard your grandchildren will feel it.

Life is what we make it, always has been, always will be.

I don't need to explain myself to you, I'm grown!

A man will only treat you how you let him.

Surround yourself with the people and things that makes you happy, forget the bad, and focus on the good.

Excuse me, excuse me from the bottom of my heart if it came out the other end it would've been a fart.

Every great dream begins with a dreamer.

Remember when I asked for your opinion? Yeah, me neither.

Hate cannot drive out hate; only love can do that.

If you can't handle my fire, let someone else enjoy the flames.

You have to be real with yourself, before you can be real with anyone else.

Oh, you're talking to me, I thought you only spoke behind my back!

When I said I'd hit that I meant with my car.

I'm not insulting you, I'm describing you.

I'm not anti-social. I'm anti-bullshit.

Don't sweat it nor regret it, just move on and forget it.

Love doesn't pay bills, unless you're a prostitute.

You know you're awesome when people you don't even know hate you.

If you have any sayings you'd like

to share email them to me at

Calls4lee@yahoo.com

Printed in Great Britain
by Amazon

27876868R00051